SUPERKIDS' CLUB
LIBRARY

D1408308

Just the Best

Written by Ann Judge and Valerie Tripp

Illustrated by Loretta Lustig and Judy DeLuca

Just the Best

<u>X</u>

six

<u>Y</u>

yell

yells

yes

yip

<u>Z</u>

zab-a-zab-zin

zab-a-zab-zub

was   you

Tac, Doc, and Oswald felt sad.

The SUPERKIDS Suns did not pick Tac, Doc, and Oswald.

Just the best kids got selected for the contest.

Just the best kids got caps and jackets.

The jackets said "SUPERKIDS Suns" on the back.

2

The SUPERKIDS Suns left for the big contest.
Oswald, Tac, and Doc felt mad.

Oswald said, "I bet the Suns
will not win the big contest."
Doc said, "I bet the Red Slicks
will stomp the Suns."
Tac said, "It is a snap for the
Red Slicks to win."

"Let's run to the big contest. Let's sit
in the stands," said Doc.
"But let's not yell for the Suns," said Oswald.
"Let's yell for the Red Slicks to win," said Tac.

Oswald, Tac, and Doc went to the big contest.

"The Red Slicks brag a lot," said Tac.

"Yes! The Red Slicks act stuck-up," said Doc.

"I can not stand it!" said Oswald. "The Red Slicks must not win! Let's help the SUPERKIDS Suns."

Tac and Doc nodded.

"The Suns did not pick us. But pals must help pals," said Doc. "Let's pep up the Suns."

It is up to us!

"Quick! Let's get back to the contest," said Doc.
Tac, Doc, Oswald, and Golly ran back to help
the SUPERKIDS Suns.

Tac, Doc, Oswald, and Golly ran in front
of the stands.
Tac held up an S.
Oswald held up a U.
Doc held up an N.
Golly held up an S.
"If you can spell it, you can yell it!" said Doc.

S-U-N-S! Suns! Suns!

The fans began to yell for the Suns.

The Suns began to grin.

Get a big hit!

Pep up, Suns!

Let's win!

The SUPERKIDS Suns began to hit runs. 1-2-3-4-5-6!

The SUPERKIDS Suns got six runs, just like the Red Slicks!

Oswald held up flags. Tac had big pom-poms.
Doc led the yells.

Zab-a-zab-zub!
Zab-a-zab-zin!
Suns! Suns! Suns!
You can win!

The fans clap and stamp and yell for the Suns.

Frits was the last of the SUPERKIDS Suns to bat.

SLAM!

Frits got a big hit!

Doc did a front flip. Oswald did a back flip. Tac did a split.

The Suns ran up to hug Oswald and Doc and Tac.
The Suns lifted up Oswald and Doc and Tac.
The Suns began to clap and yell.

Yip! Yip! Yip!

Oswald is just the best!
Doc is just the best!
Tac is just the best!

Oswald and Doc and Tac felt grand. It was just the best!

SUPERKIDS' CLUB
LIBRARY

Frits Had a Frog

The Sled Dog

A Hat for Alf

Across the Desert

Drip! Drop!

The Fitness Test

The Skunk on the Bus

Top Dog

The Gifts

Just the Best